WE'RE GOING TO FIND THE STER!

Written by
MALORIE BLACKMAN

Illustrated by
DAPO ADEOLA

PUFFIN

For Neil and Liz, with love. And to all the young at heart,
in celebration of family and imagination – M.B.

For my Goddaughter Princess Madison and my Godson Truce:
may your adventures always keep you several steps
ahead of any monsters X – D.A.

PUFFIN BOOKS

UK | USA | Canada | Ireland | Australia | India | New Zealand | South Africa

Puffin Books is part of the Penguin Random House group of companies
whose addresses can be found at global.penguinrandomhouse.com.

First published 2021

004

Printed in China

The authorized representative in the EEA is Penguin Random House Ireland,
Morrison Chambers, 32 Nassau Street, Dublin D02 YH68

A CIP catalogue record for this book is available from the British Library

ISBN: 978–0–241–40130–9

All correspondence to: Puffin Books, Penguin Random House Children's
One Embassy Gardens, 8 Viaduct Gardens, London SW11 7BW

MIX
Paper from
responsible sources
FSC
www.fsc.org
FSC® C018179

Charlie and Eddie were playing in the garden.
"Breakfast in ten minutes," called Dad.

"Come on!" said Charlie.
   "We need to find the monster!"

"But it's breakfast time. He'll be grumpy," said Eddie.

"He'll be grumpy and hungry," said Charlie.

"He'll be grumpy and hungry and snappy!" said Eddie.

"He'll be **grumpy** and **hungry** and **snappy** and **prickly!**"
they both said together.

"shhh!
We'll need to be
very careful!"

And off they went.

"We're going to find the **monster!**"

They sailed over a **shimmering ocean**.

"Look out!

There's a whale!" Eddie pointed.

"No problem!" said Charlie.
And she rowed their boat quickly round it.

"Over the **shimmering ocean** . . .
We're going to find the **monster!**"

They began to climb a **huge, high mountain**.

"Look out!
A hungry wolf!"

"Don't worry!"
said Charlie.

And she sang a soft, sweet song to soothe it.
Then she gave it a massive hug and sent it on its way.

"Over the **shimmering ocean** . . .

Up the **huge, high mountain** . . .

We're going to find the **monster!**"

They crept through a
deep, dark jungle . . .

"**Look out!**
A fearsome, fierce tiger,"
said Eddie.

They hid in a cave, but only just in time!

The most fearsome, fierce tiger
in the whole world slunk past.

Eddie and Charlie held their breath
until it had gone. **"Phew! That was close!"**

They floated in giant bubbles across the bubbly bubble lake, careful not to disturb the foamy fiend.

Luckily it was too busy relaxing to notice them!

"Over the **shimmering ocean** . . .

Up the **huge, high mountain** . . .

Through the **deep, dark jungle** . . .

Across the **bubbly bubble lake** . . .

We're going to find the **monster!**"

"Ooh! This is the smelliest, messiest, scariest place in the WHOLE WIDE WORLD!"

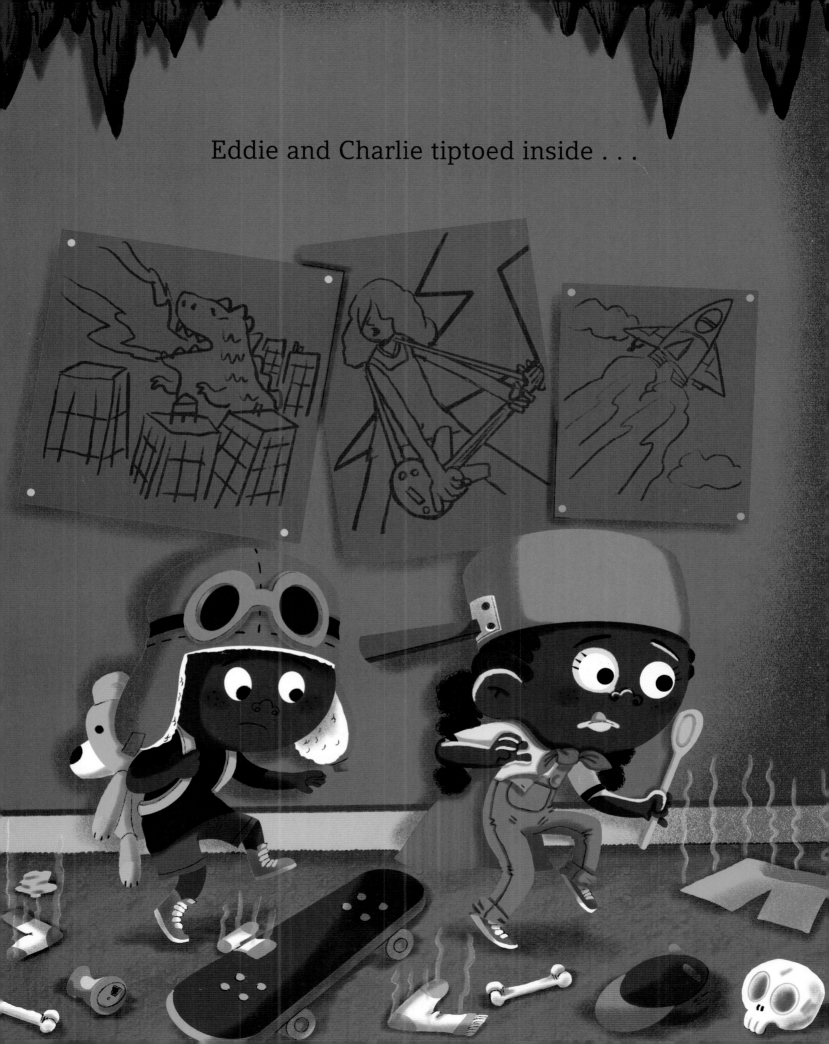

Eddie and Charlie tiptoed inside . . .

And there it was . . .

the Monster!

The monster was fast asleep and snoring his head off.

"Let's get him!" whispered Eddie.

Charlie crept up to the **monster** . . .

"Breakfast time!" she shouted.

The **monster** sprang up.

"RAAARRGGHH!"

he roared. **"Tickle time!"**

And he chased Eddie and Charlie out of his lair . . .

. . . past the **foamy fiend**,

around the **fearsome, fierce tiger**,

over the **hungry wolf**,

down,

down,

down

the **huge, high mountain,**

beyond the **shimmering ocean . . .**

. . . and into the kitchen – where a breakfast
of yummies was waiting for them.

The **monster** grabbed Charlie and tickled her tummy.
Then he snatched up Eddie and tickled him too.

"Marcus, stop tickling your brother and sister and sit down for breakfast!" said Dad.

"And if I don't?" laughed Marcus.

And that's exactly what they did!